FOR FATHER
with love

Edited by Helen Exley

⑤EXLEY

In the same series:
For Grandad, a gift of love
For Mother, a gift of love
Love, a celebration
Love, a keepsake
Love is a grandmother
Marriage, a keepsake
Thank Heavens for friends

Published in Great Britain in 1985 by
Exley Publications Ltd,
16 Chalk Hill, Watford, Herts WD1 4BN, United Kingdom.

Second printing 1986
Third printing 1989
Fourth & fifth printings 1990

Selection and design: © Helen and Richard Exley, 1985
ISBN 1-85015-024-9

Typeset by Brush Off Studios, St Albans, Herts.
Printed and bound in Hungary.

DISTRIBUTED BY
Pam's Den INC.
P.O. BOX 1231, LAMBETH
ONTARIO N0L 1S0

I would like to dedicate this book to my dad, Tor, who died unexpectedly during its preparation leaving so much unsaid and so much undone. If only I had flown out earlier, especially to see him; instead I flew to his funeral ... If only the book had been ready to give to him ...
And to Richard, my husband, father of my boys —
you are the kindest dad I have ever seen — never forget that.

My thanks go to Margaret Montgomery and Jane Varley who rescued the book when it was running late. And also to Pam Brown, who trudged around countless libraries to find father poems for me and then herself wrote some of the best pieces in the book.

DEFINITIONS OF A FATHER

The final judge of every man is his child.

Fatherhood precipitates many men into a desperate scramble to grow up over night.

Dads either know too little about the subject on which you have to write an essay — or far, far, *far* too much.

A father is the man who lies awake worrying about the spanking he's given his child when the child has forgotten it and gone to sleep.

Children give their fathers the chance to be the man they would have liked to be. For a little while.

We are finally grown up when we can forgive our parents.

You worship him as a hero, then despise him as a man. Eventually you love him as a human being.

It's easy, when your child believes you are always right, to slip into believing it's the truth.

Pam Brown

If you live without being a father you will die
without being a human being.

Russian proverb

If a man smiles at home somebody is sure to ask
him for money.

William Feather

There has been a succession of women's revolutions
in America. But watch out for the revolt of the
father, if he should get fed up with feeding others,
and get bored with being used, and lay down his
tools, and walk off to consult his soul.

Max Lerner

We think of a father as an old, or at least a middle-
aged man. The astounding truth is that most fathers
are young men, and that they make their greatest
sacrifices in their youth. I never meet a young man
on Sunday morning wheeling along his first baby
without feeling an ache of reverence.

James Douglas

No man can possibly know what life means, what
the world means, what anything means, until he has
a child and loves it. And then the whole universe
changes and nothing will ever again seem exactly as
it seemed before.

Lafcadio Hearn

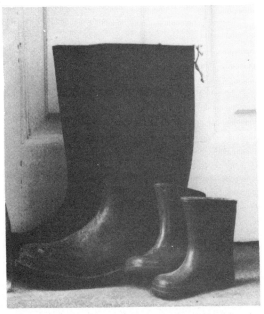

One word of command from me is obeyed by millions . . . but I cannot get my three daughters, Pamela, Felicity and Joan, to come down to breakfast on time.

Viscount Archibald Wavell

The first service a child does his father is to make him foolish.

English proverb

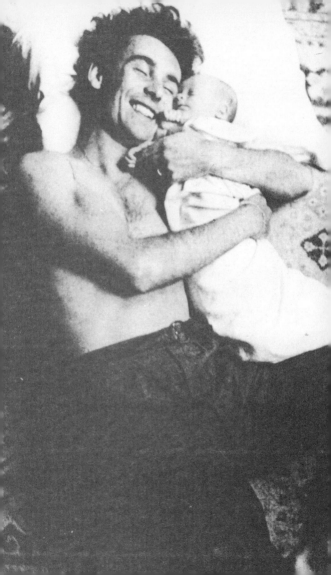

Last night my child was born — a very strong boy, with large black eyes. . . If you ever become a father, I think the strangest and strongest sensation of your life will be hearing for the first time the thin cry of your own child. For a moment you have the strange feeling of being double; but there is something more, quite impossible to analyze — perhaps the echo in a man's heart of all the sensations felt by all the fathers and mothers of his race at a similar instant in the past. It is a very tender, but also a very ghostly feeling.

Lafcadio Hearn

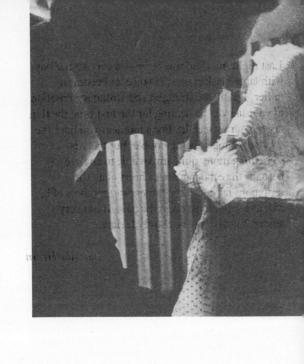

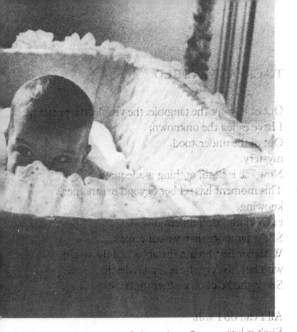

When one becomes a father, then first one becomes a son. Standing by the crib of one's own baby, with that world-old pang of compassion and protectiveness toward this so little creature that has all its course to run, the heart flies back in yearning and gratitude to those who felt just so towards one's self. Then for the first time one understands the homely succession of sacrifices and pains by which life is transmitted and fostered down the stumbling generations of men.

Christopher Morley

TO CREATE A CHILD

Out of love for the tangible, the visible, the present,
I have called the unknown;
Out of the understood,
mystery.
Now she is flesh, nothing is adequate.
This moment has set her beyond her mother's
knowing,
beyond my comprehension.
She is far more than we conceived.
With her first breath she absorbed the world,
with her first cry she accepted death.
She is the heart of another universe.

All I can do I will;
Shelter her,
teach her,
love her,
learn each day something of what she is.

But never again in utter confidence.
Never again unafraid.
She, in her vulnerability,
reveals the dangers of the dark.

Peter Gray

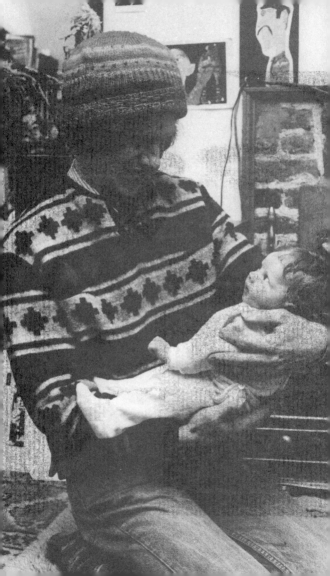

This nothing-much boy,
this acne-haunted lad,
has, by incompetence,
become a dad:
cradles his newborn child,
afraid to move,
and, in bewilderment,
discovers love.

Pamela Brown

SOLILOQUY IN CIRCLES

Being a father
Is quite a bother.

You are free as air
With time to spare,

You're a fiscal rocket
With change in your pocket,

And then one morn
A child is born.

Your life has been runcible,
Irresponsible,

Like an arrow or javelin
You've been constantly travelin',

But mostly, I daresay,
Without a *chaise percée*,

To which by comparison
Nothing's embarison.

But all children matures,
Maybe even yours.

You improve them mentally
And straighten them dentally,

They grow tall as a lancer
And ask questions you can't answer,

And supply you with data
About how everybody else wears lipstick
   sooner and stays up later,

And if they are popular,
The phone they monopular.

They scorn the dominion
Of their parent's opinion,

They're no longer corralable
Once they find that you're fallible.

But after you've raised them
   and educated them and gowned them,
They just take their little fingers
   and wrap you around them.

Being a father
Is quite a bother,
But I like it, rather.

Ogden Nash

IN THE SERVICE OF THE EMPRESS

MY wife and I, we entered domestic service five weeks ago. It is much as we expected it would be. We spend much of our time in the kitchen now, muttering in the way of servants whenever an intermission occurs between the imperious yells.

Like most dictators, our employer seems to find it difficult distinguishing between day and night. She sleeps in the day but then in the small hours or at dawn the summons comes, just as Hitler's and Stalin's came, to send feet clattering across the halls of serpentine and syenite.

But so far we have been spared the monologues about the New Order. New Orders do not interest her, for she has gone back beyond all ordered society to a state of egomania that not even dictators know. One blue eye opens, and there must be food; it shuts, and there must be warmth. If either is lacking, all hell breaks loose.

As servants, we are out of the reach of any trade union. We have gone back, too, beyond serfdom and slavery, to the wood and the moon. However much we mutter, we know we are in the service of a living god and there is nothing we can do about it. When last measured the god was 22 inches long.

Byron Rogers

What a father says to his children is not heard by the world, but it will be heard by posterity.

Jean Paul Richter

Abstracted from home, I know no happiness in this world.

Thomas Jefferson

What do I owe my father? Everything.

Henry van Dyke

You see that boy of mine? Though but five, he governs the universe. Yes, for he rules his mother, his mother rules me, I rule Athens, and Athens the world.

Themistocles

If I were asked to name the world's greatest need, I should say unhesitatingly; wise mothers and . . . exemplary fathers.

David O. McKay

He is the happiest, be he king or peasant, who finds peace in his home.

Johann Wolfgang von Goethe

When bairns are young they gar their parents' head ache;
When they are auld they make their hearts ache.

Scottish proverb

A thoughtful father will always offer in a kindly,
loving, sleepy voice, to feed and change the baby.
Just as his wife is climbing back into bed.

Pamela Dugdale

Don't blame your parents. They didn't choose
you either.

Alexander Pola

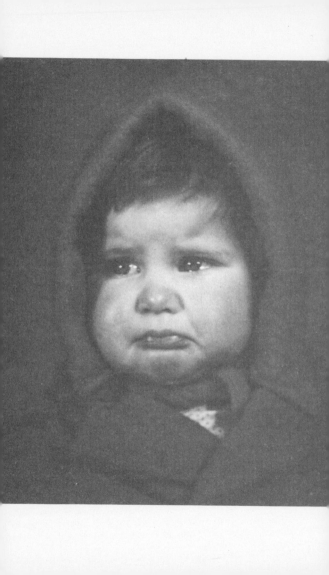

THE JUDGE

Say of him what you please, but I know my child's failings.

I do not love him because he is good, but because
he is my little child.

How should you know how dear he can be when you try to weigh his merits against his faults?

When I must punish him, he becomes all the more a part of my being.

When I cause his tears to come, my heart weeps with him.

I alone have a right to blame and punish, for he only may chastise who loves.

Rabindranath Tagore

. . . For who knows what my girl will be? She's only a few months old, and a surprise already — and I imagine I've just got a lot more surprises coming. But in the end, I suppose, I just want to give her love and the assurance of a home on earth. This child was not born merely to extend my ego, nor even to give me unbroken pleasure, nor to provide me with a plaything to be fussed over, neglected, shown off and then put away. She was born that I might give her a first foot in this world and might help her to want to live in it. She is here through me, and I am responsible for her — and I'm not looking for any escape-clauses there. Having a child alters the rights of every man, and I don't expect to live as I did without her. I am hers to be with, and hope to be what she needs, and know of no reason why I should ever desert her.

Laurie Lee

A FATHER'S HAPPINESS

To show a child what has once delighted you, to find the child's delight added to your own, so that there is now a double delight seen in the glow of trust and affection, this is happiness.

J. B. Priestley

NICER THAN HUMANS

Children are corks
Exploding suddenly during heat-waves;
Hosepipes gone mad
Spraying us with cold water;
Going off behind our backs
Like rip-raps
They assault our world with clowning.

They are tough as whipcord
And as easily swayed
As gossamer, lightly hurt
As dandelion clocks;
Repetitious as pod-peas;
Maddening as flies;
Direct as nudity;
Unhinged as moths at night yet wise
As old roads and buried tracks can be;
They seem to belong
To an earlier species,
Imbued with the fragility of pure spirit
In bodies of india-rubber.

We have no defence
Against their wiles;
With innocent faces, ice-cream smiles.

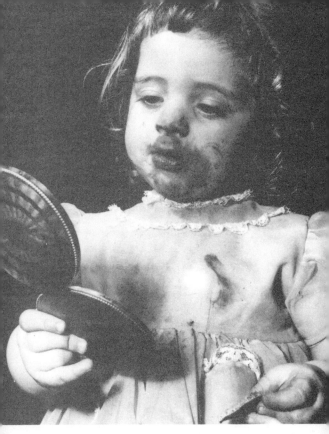

As Milligan said
In a goonish quip,
So much nicer than human beings!

John Barron Mays

THE FATHER'S SONG

Great snowslide,
Stay away from my igloo,
I have my four children and my wife;
They can never enrich you.

Strong snowslide,
Roll past my weak house.
There sleep my dear ones in the world.
Snowslide, let their night be calm.

Sinister snowslide,
I just built an igloo here, sheltered from the wind.
It is my fault if it is put wrong.
Snowslide, hear me from your mountain.

Greedy snowslide,
There is enough to smash and smother.
Fall down over the ice,
Bury stones and cliffs and rocks.

Snowslide, I own so little in the world.
Keep away from my igloo, stop not our travels.
Nothing will you gain by our horror and death,
Mighty snowslide, mighty snowslide.

Little snowslide,
Four children and my wife are my whole world, all
   I own,
All I can lose, nothing can you gain.
Snowslide, save my house, stay on your summit.

Eskimo prayer

TO MY DAUGHTER

Bright clasp of her whole hand around my finger,
My daughter, as we walk together now.
All my life I'll feel a ring invisibly
Circle this bone with shining: when she is grown
Far from today as her eyes are far already.

Stephen Spender

Only a father would ride on the rollercoaster with me, come off with a green face and say he had a good time.

Loni Casale, age 11

A father is for being talked into being a butterfly in my school play.

Robin Rosenbalm, age 11

A dad is a person that thinks he knows everything but doesn't even understand simple new math.

Melissa Wellington, age 10

A father is a person that puts things off so he can put them off next week again.

Jimmy Athens, age 11

I like my dad, because when I was five he would play football. But now he can't play football, because he's thirty.

Theron Carnell, age 9

A father is someone who will tell your mother, on her birthday, that *you* picked out all the presents when you had forgotten is *was* her birthday.

Raymond Angell, age 14

A father is the type of person who says he is eating all of your birthday chocolates so you won't get fillings in your teeth.

Leslie Roles, age 13

Sometimes when he gets mad at me I can understand why.

Michelle Walsh, age 13

A dad is somebody who can get away with doing things he tells you not to do.

Paul Raiche, age 14

I was born because I wanted to be like my dad.

Samuel Lin

GIRL'S-EYE VIEW OF RELATIVES

The thing to remember about fathers is, they're men.
A girl has to keep it in mind.
They are dragon-seekers, bent on improbable
    rescues.
Scratch any father, you find
Someone chock-full of qualms and romantic terrors,
Believing change is a threat —
Like your first shoes with heels on, like your first
    bicycle
It took such months to get.

Walk in strange woods, they warn you about the
    snakes there.
Climb, and they fear you'll fall.
Books, angular boys, or swimming in deep water —
Fathers mistrust them all.
Men are the worriers. It is difficult for them
To learn what they must learn:
How you have a journey to take and very likely,
For a while, will not return.

Phyllis McGinley

THE THINGS MY CHILDREN
TAUGHT ME

One of the best things about children is their
humanizing influence. You have to deal with them
on their level. You cannot impress them with your
title or your prestige or your bluster. You cannot
hide from them. You have to relate to them directly
as people, and that is something many of us don't
do very often. Talk about reducing life to
simplicities! Trying to communicate with a child is
one of the simplest acts imaginable. Just the two of
you. When it's not driving you crazy ("Why?"
"Because. . .") it can be wonderfully refreshing.

Most of all, children teach the capacity for
enjoyment. The ecstasy a child can find in a carrot
or an apple is simply amazing. They like to run just
for the fun of it, or stick their heads out the window
of the car to feel the wind. They can break through
all those levels of control, all those accretions of
detachment and sobriety that plug up your laugh
ducts. When I come home at night and the two of
them burst through the door, running down the
walk to greet me, the world is a beautiful place. No
matter what else has happened, it's beautiful.

When you are really in love, you think you are
the first person who has ever felt that way.
Parenthood should be the same way. I don't care if

it's trite — I love to hear my children laugh, just as
I love to see my wife standing in the doorway,
watching us.

Steven V. Roberts.

RUNNING CHILD

Watching my running child
On her seventh summer's beach
I see that other child
Incredulously allowed back
Through the afternoon's haze
To run beside her
Turning his head towards her
To gauge his joy

Thirty years ago

Don Coles

IN PRAISE OF FATHERS

In the baby lies the future of the world.
Mother must hold the baby close so that
the baby knows it is his world but father
must take him to the highest hill so that he
can see what his world is like.

A Mayan Indian proverb

FATHER SAYS

Father says
Never
let
me
see
you
doing
that
again
father says
tell you once
tell you a thousand times
come hell or high water
his finger drills my shoulder
never let me see you doing that again

My brother knows all his phrases off by heart
so we practice them in bed at night.

Michael Rosen

FOR A FATHER

With the exact length and pace of his father's
    stride
The son walks,
Echoes and intonations of his father's speech
Are heard when he talks.

Once when the table was tall,
And the chair a wood
He absorbed his father's smile and carefully
    copied
The way he stood.

He grew into exile slowly,
With pride and remorse,
In some way better than his begetters,
In others worse.

And now having chosen, with strangers,
Half glad of his choice,
He smiles with his father's hesitant smile
And speaks with his voice.

Anthony Cronin

NOW THAT YOUR SHOULDERS REACH MY SHOULDERS

My shoulders once were yours for riding.
My feet were yours for walking, wading.
My morning once was yours for taking.

Still I can almost feel the pressure
Of your warm hands clasping my forehead
While my hands grasped your willing ankles.

Now that your shoulders reach my shoulders
What is there left for me to give you?
Where is a weight to lift as welcome?

Robert Francis

"YOU DON'T *HAVE* TO PAY"

"Hello, I have a collect call from Miss Joyce Robinson in Oshkosh, Wisconsin. Will you accept the charges?"

"Yes, operator, we will."

"Hi, Pops. How are you?"

"Fine. What are you doing in Oshkosh? I thought you were driving to Cape Cod to visit Aunt Rose."

"We were, but Cynthia wanted to stop off and visit a boy she knew from school who lives in Minneapolis."

"Who is Cynthia?"

"She's a girl I met in New Orleans."

"New Orleans? I didn't know you went to New Orleans."

"I wasn't planning to, but Tommy said there was a great concert of the Grateful Dead scheduled to play in the stadium. He got the day right, but the wrong month."

"Tommy?"

"He was hitch-hiking on Ninety-five."

"You started out with Ellen Mulberry. Where is she?"

"She met some kids she knew in Fort Lauderdale, and they were driving to Mexico, so she decided to go with them."

"Do Mr. and Mrs. Mulberry know this?"

"I think Ellen called them after the accident."

"What accident?"

"The camper she was in had a blowout, and Ellen got banged up a little."

"So you're now traveling with Cynthia and Tommy."

"No. Tommy stayed in New Orleans, and Cynthia left yesterday. She said she couldn't wait until my car was fixed."

"What's wrong with your car?"

"The motor fell out. That's what I'm calling you about. The garageman said it will cost five hundred and fifty dollars to fix it up."

"That's a fortune!"

"You don't have to pay it if you don't want to. I can leave the car here. I met a guy who has a motorcycle, and he says he'll take me as far as Detroit."

"I'LL PAY IT!"

"How's Mom?"

"She's on the extension. I think she was fine until we got your call. Where are you staying until you get your car fixed?"

"I met some nice kids who have a religious commune near here, and they said I could stay with them if I promise to devote the rest of my life to God."

"That's nice."

"The only problem is I have to shave my head."

"Can't you stay at a motel?"

"I don't have any money left."

"What happened to the three hundred dollars I gave you?"

"Two hundred went for expenses, and one

hundred of it went for the fine."

"What fine?"

"We were fined one hundred dollars for speeding in this little itty-bitty town in Arkansas."

"I told you not to drive fast."

"I wasn't driving. Fred was."

"Who the hell is Fred?"

"He's a vegetarian, and he says capitalism is finished in the West."

"That's worth one hundred dollars to hear. Are you going to Cape Cod to visit Aunt Rose or aren't you?"

"As soon as I get the car fixed, Pops. Send me the money care of Western Union. You don't want the man to fix the dented door at the same time?"

"Your car had no dented door."

"It does now. I have to go, Dad. Some kids I met are going to take me white-water canoeing. Good-bye. And, Pops — have a nice day."

Art Buchwald

IF —

If you can keep your head when all about you
    Are losing theirs and blaming it on you;
If you can trust yourself when all men doubt you,
    But make allowance for their doubting too;
If you can wait and not be tired by waiting,
    Or, being lied about, don't deal in lies,
Or, being hated, don't give way to hating,
    And yet don't look too good, nor talk too wise;

If you can dream — and not make dreams your master;
    If you can think — and not make thoughts your aim;
If you can meet with triumph and disaster
    And treat those two impostors just the same;
If you can bear to hear the truth you've spoken
    Twisted by knaves to make a trap for fools,
Or watch the things you gave your life to broken,
    And stoop and build 'em up with worn out tools;

If you can make one heap of all your winnings
    And risk it on one turn of pitch-and-toss,
And lose, and start again at your beginnings
    And never breathe a word about your loss;
If you can force your heart and nerve and sinew
    To serve your turn long after they are gone,
And so hold on when there is nothing in you
    Except the Will which says to them: 'Hold on';

If you can talk with crowds and keep your virtue,
    Or walk with kings — nor lose the common touch;
If neither foes nor loving friends can hurt you;
    If all men count with you, but none too much;
If you can fill the unforgiving minute
    With sixty seconds' worth of distance run —
Yours is the Earth and everything that's in it,
    And — which is more — you'll be a Man, my son!

                                    Rudyard Kipling

JESSY

As she has grown as a daughter, so have I grown as
a father, and have learned to bury away my wishful
images of her, to watch her take charge of her own
directions and to develop her own dependence and
will.

True, in the beginning she showed certain
promising tendrils — early soppiness about the
moon, an especially fine touch on the piano, and an
unquestioning belief in my faultlessness. But these
shoots withered soon; she never quite finished her
first-year Mozart, began to find the moon-rise a bit
of a bore, and though ready to be guided by me on
her choice of chocolate bars, gradually came to the
conclusion, as her eyes grew level with mine, that I
was really a bit of a joke.

So what I've got in the place of my early self-
indulgencies is not the compliant doll of an old
dad's fantasy, but a glowing girl with a dazzling and
complicated personality, one with immense energy
in the pursuit of happiness and despair, who
expresses her love for me, not in secret half-smiles,
or in an intimate sharing of silences, but in noisy
shouts, happy punches, and hungry burying of
teeth in my ear-lobes.

Certainly she is no daddy's soft shadow, nor ever
will be; she exists on a different scale to my first

fond imaginings. She is at last herself, a normal, jeans-clad, horse-riding, pop-swinging, piano-bashing girl with a huge appetite for the creamier pleasures of life.

Not at all what I planned, or what I expected, but I don't think I would exchange her for anything else.

Laurie Lee

NEARING MANHOOD

A father sees a son nearing manhood.
What shall he tell that son?
"Life is hard; be steel; be a rock."
And this might stand him for the storms
and serve him for humdrum and monotony
and guide him amid sudden betrayals
and tighten him for slack moments.
"Life is a soft loam; be gentle; go easy."
And this too might serve him.
Brutes have been gentled where lashes failed.
The growth of a frail flower in a path up
has sometimes shattered and split a rock.
A tough will counts. So does desire.
So does a rich soft wanting.
Without rich wanting nothing arrives.
Tell him too much money has killed men
and left them dead years before burial:
the quest of lucre beyond a few easy needs
has twisted good enough men
sometimes into dry thwarted worms.
Tell him time as a stuff can be wasted.
Tell him to be a fool every so often
and to have no shame over having been a fool
yet learning something out of every folly
hoping to repeat none of the cheap follies
thus arriving at intimate understanding
of a world numbering many fools.

Tell him to be alone often and get at himself
and above all tell himself no lies about himself
whatever the white lies and protective fronts
he may use amongst other people.
Tell him solitude is creative if he is strong
and the final decisions are made in silent rooms.
Tell him to be different from other people
if it comes natural and easy being different.
Let him have lazy days seeking his deeper motives.
Let him seek deep for where his is a born natural.
    Then he may understand Shakespeare
    and the Wright brothers, Pasteur, Pavlov,
    Michael Faraday and free imaginations
bringing changes into a world resenting change.
    He will be lonely enough
    to have time for the work
    he knows as his own.

                                    Carl Sandburg

APOLOGY

"Sorry" seems inadequate.
"I never meant it", fatuous.
And it's too late for tears.
How then to tell you all I've learned these twenty
    years?
I stand here in the cold December day
and thrust a gift-wrapped parcel at your chest
and say
"Best love from all of us.
A happy birthday, Dad."

A box of time remembered.

The same late gift you gave your father once
. . . and he to his.

Pamela Brown

THE PRODIGAL SON

And he said, "There was a man who had two sons; and the younger of them said to his father, 'Father, give me the share of property that falls to me.' And he divided his living between them. Not many days later, the younger son gathered all he had and took his journey into a far country, and there he squandered his property in loose living. And when he had spent everything, a great famine arose in that country, and he began to be in want. So he went and joined himself to one of the citizens of that country, who sent him into his fields to feed swine. And he would gladly have fed on the pods that the swine ate; and no one gave him anything. But when he came to himself he said, 'How many of my father's hired servants have bread enough and to spare, but I perish here with hunger. I will arise and go to my father, and I will say to him, "Father, I have sinned against heaven and before you; I am no longer worthy to be called your son; treat me as one of your hired servants."' And he arose and came to his father. But while he was yet at a distance, his father saw him and had compassion and ran and embraced him and kissed him. And the son said to him, 'Father, I have sinned against heaven and before you; I am no longer worthy to be called your son.' But the father said to his servants,

'Bring quickly the best robe, and put it on him; and put a ring on his hand, and shoes on his feet; and bring the fatted calf and kill it and let us eat and make merry; for this my son was dead, and is alive again; he was lost, and is found.' And they began to make merry.

"Now his elder son was in the field; and as he came and drew near to the house, he heard music and dancing. And he called one of the servants and asked what this meant. And he said to him, 'Your brother has come, and your father has killed the fatted calf, because he has received him safe and sound.' But he was angry and refused to go in. His father came out and entreated him, but he answered his father, 'Lo, these many years I have served you, and I never disobeyed your command; yet you never gave me a kid, that I might make merry with my friends. But when this son of yours came, who has devoured your living with harlots, you killed for him the fatted calf!' And he said to him, 'Son, you are always with me, and all that is mine is yours. It was fitting to make merry and be glad, for this your brother was dead, and is alive; he was lost, and is found.' "

From Luke, Chapter 15, The Bible

POLONIUS GIVES HIS SON LAERTES
SOME SOUND ADVICE

Polonius: Give thy thoughts no tongue,
Nor any unproportioned thought his act.
Be thou familiar, but by no means vulgar.
The friends thou hast, and their adoption tried,
Grapple them to thy soul with hoops of steel;
But do not dull thy palm with entertainment
Of each new-hatched, unfledged comrade. Beware
Of entrance to a quarrel; but being in,
Bear't, that th'opposed may beware of thee.
Give every man thine ear, but few thy voice;
Take each man's censure, but reserve thy judgement.
Costly thy habit as thy purse can buy,
But not expressed in fancy; rich, not gaudy;
For the apparel oft proclaims the man . . .
Neither a borrower, nor a lender be,
For loan oft loses both itself and friend,
And borrowing dulls the edge of husbandry.
This above all: to thine own self be true,
And it must follow, as the night the day,
Thou canst not then be false to any man.

William Shakespeare 'Hamlet'

At twenty he had put on this costume of
fatherhood, padded the shoulders, added to his
height, deepened his voice to fit the part. I never
saw the greasepaint or the wig line as I clasped his
hand.

Only when I had grown and had
come to know everything myself, did I see the
fraud. A well intentioned man, but not the man I
thought him. A little man. A man who blurred into
the small suburban landscape, his friends as
nondescript and kind as he, his work respectable,
ambition long since burned away. I saw him so till
now, but suddenly I find him changed. Years and
indifference have made him careless. He forsook
the padding and the heels somewhere along the
way, but how could this diminish his reality? He is,

I see, himself. Not shrunken, but the man he was before we came. His voice has lifted. His eyes are more alert, no longer speaking of preoccupations with children's shoes and adolescent brushes with the Law.

He has taken up again the things we interrupted, the skills we crowded to the edges of his life. He is no longer obliged to steal time for himself. We are his companions now, his friends, rather than demanding voices always at his elbow.

He has not grown young again. I see now that he was never old. The painted wrinkles that he still retains, the careful silver streaks, no longer fool us. My dad's a man as young as any of his children.

Perhaps a little younger.

Charlotte Gray

BEFORE IT GETS TOO LATE, DAD

Poets are inclined to weep
when their papas are buried deep,
tucked up and out of sight.
They wallow in complete recall,
which doesn't help their dads at all,
or make the wrong things right.
But I'm no poet, so I'll say
all my apologies today
for every teenage fight,
for every laziness and lie,
for every bitterness and sigh
I caused you. . . . Better live than write,
old love; we'll use our days
in daft, companionable ways
while we've still life and light.

Pamela Brown

MY FATHER

I took my father for granted,
never thought him courageous,
A clean watchful man
who never raised his voice;
never stood at a barricade
but quietly held his course.
Never unjust to the young,
never betrayed his trust.
Secret in his love.

Now I know
the small disciplines of day by day,
spoke for a valiant heart.

Henry Chapin

One moment's obedience to natural law and an ordinary man finds himself called upon to be wise, kindly, patient, loving, dispenser of justice, arbiter of truth, consultant paediatrician, expert in education, financial wizard, mender of toys, source of all knowledge, master of skills.

And to wake one day to find that he has failed and that he is, after all, a silly old devil who's out of touch and out of date. He should not be discouraged. He will eventually be reinstated.

Peter Gray

STANZAS FOR MY DAUGHTER

Tell her I love
   she will remember me
always, for she
is of love's graces made;
   she will remember
these streets where the moon's shade
falls and my shadow mingles
with shadows sprung
from a midnight tree.

Tell her I love that I
am neither in cloud nor sky,
stone nor cloud,
but only this
walled garden she knows well
and which her body is.

Her eyes alone shall make
me blossom for her sake;
contained within her, all
my days shall flower or die,
birthday or funeral
concealed where no man's eye
finds me unless she says:
He is my flesh and I
am what he was.

Horace Gregory

FATHER

Your coughing hurts me more. On winter mornings
And coming up the road it is your sign.
I see at last that you are growing old.
This summer you retired. Whose life with mine
Was mingled for so long and never noticed
More than as the flavour of a coat
Smelling of tobacco, as a forehead
Frowning at the desk-top where you wrote
Figures in a black book, adding up
To everything, to nothing, to a wage —
I whose youth so took your love for granted,
What answer can I make now to your age?

Father, it is too late. I want for you
All the chances that were never yours,
Summer. . . but what can come? Only the summer
That autumn brings, the days warm for five hours
After the mist clears, and before the sunset.
Father, then I want for you no less.
Here in the autumn garden where you sit
Unlearning slowly an old restlessness,
Red admirals still tremble on the stonecrop,
While swallows come, as to a meeting-place.
Read now, remember, watch your children's children,
And fall asleep with sunlight on your face.

David Sutton

ACKNOWLEDGEMENTS: The publishers gratefully acknowledge permission to reproduce copyright material. Every effort has been made to trace copyright holders, but in a few cases this has proved impossible. The publishers would be interested to hear from any copyright holders not here acknowledged.

ART BUCHWALD, "You don't have to pay" (originally titled "Collect Call") from *Washington is Leaking.* Copyright © 1976 by Art Buchwald. Reprinted by permission of Putnam Publishing Group, New York; HENRY CHAPIN, "My father" from *The Haunt of Time.* Copyright © 1981 William L. Bauhan, Publisher, Dublin, N.H.; DON COLES, "Running Child" from *Anniversaries.* Reprinted by permission of Macmillan of Canada, A Division of Canada Publishing Corporation; ANTHONY CRONIN, "For a father", from *New and Selected Poems,* published by Carcanet, Manchester. Copyright © 1982 Anthony Cronin; "For a Father", from *New and Selected Poems,* published by Carcanet, Manchester. Copyright © 1982 Anthony Cronin; ROBERT FRANCIS, "My shoulders once were yours for riding" from *Collected Poems: 1936-1976,* copyright 1936, 1967 by Robert Francis. Reprinted by permission of The University of Massachusetts Press; PETER FREUCHEN (translator), "The father's song" from *Book of the Eskimos.* Reprinted by permission of Harold Matson Company Inc.; HORACE GREGORY, "Stanzas for my daughter" from *Collected Poems* by Horace Gregory. Copyright © 1964 by Horace Gregory. Reprinted by permission of Holt, Rinehart and Winston, Publishers and Harold Matson Company, Inc.; LAFCADIO HEARN, extracts from *Life and Letters* edited by Elizabeth Bisland, 1906; RUDYARD KIPLING, "If" from Rudyard Kipling Verse, definitive edition. Copyright © 1910 by Doubleday Inc. Used by permission of The National Tust, the Macmillan Company of London and Basingstoke and Doubleday Inc, New York; LAURIE LEE, extracts from *I Can't Stay Long,* reprinted by permission of André Deutsch and Atheneum Publishers; LUKE chapter 15 vv 11-32 from the Revised Standard Version of the Bible, copyright 1946, 1952 © 1971, 1973, by permission of the National Council of the Churches of Christ; JOHN BARRON MAYS, "Nicer than humans". Reprinted by permission of Enitharmon Press; PHYLLIS McGINLEY, "Girl's-Eye View of Relatives", from *Times Three.* Copyright © 1959 by Phyllis McGinley. Originally published in the New Yorker. Reprinted by permission of Viking Penguin Inc., New York and Martin Secker and Warburg Limited; CHRISTOPHER MORLEY, extract from "Mince Pie", reprinted by permission of Harper & Row Publishers Inc.; OGDEN NASH, "The Parent" and "Soliloquy in Circles" from *Verses from 1929 On* Copyright © 1933. 1948, 1956, renewed 1983, by Ogden Nash. Reprinted by permission of Curtis Brown, Ltd. London and New York and Little, Brown and Company, Boston; J. B. PRIESTLEY, "A father's happiness". Reprinted by permission of William Heinemann Ltd.; STEVEN V. ROBERTS, "The things my children taught me" from *Confessions of a Confirmed Father,* originally published in Redbook Magazine; BYRON ROGERS, extract from "In the service of the empress", first published in The Sunday Times 18 September 1983. By permission of Times Newspapers Limited; MICHAEL ROSEN, "Father says" from *Mind Your Own Business.* Reprinted by permission of André Deutsch; CARL SANDBURG from *The People, Yes* by Carl

Gift books from Exley Publications:

Love, a Keepsake. £4.99. Writers and poets old and new have captured the feeling of being in love, in this very personal collection. Specially designed as a lover's gift, bound in pale blue suedel.

Love, a Celebration. £4.99. Bound in burgundy suedel, this is a gift for someone special in your life. A selection of poems and prose by great writers celebrates the joys and wonders of love.

Marriage, a Keepsake. £4.99. With a silvery suedel cover, this collection of poems and prose contains some of the finest love messages between husbands and wives. For all couples from those about to marry to those who have known many good years together.

Thank Heavens for Friends. £4.99. The most precious thing in all the world is a really good friend. This collection, bound in pale green suedel, is a perfect gift for a friend you truly cherish.

For Mother, a gift of love. £4.99. Bound in dusky blue suedel, this collection of tributes includes such great writers as Victor Hugo and Tennyson. A perfect gift for Mother's day – or any other!

For Father, with love. £4.99. Show your father how much you appreciate him. Handsomely bound in brown suedel, this is a gift he will keep and treasure.

Love is a Grandmother. £4.99. "Everyone should have one, especially if you don't have TV, because grandmothers are the only grown-ups who have the time!" This anthology is bound in soft beige suedel.

For Granddad, a gift of love. £4.99. This charming selection reflects the special bond between grandfather and grandchild. Handsomely bound in chocolate brown suedel.

United Kingdom: Order these books from your local bookseller or from Exley Publications Ltd, Dept BP, 16 Chalk Hill, Watford, Herts WD1 4BN. (Please send £1.00 to cover post and packing.)

United States: All these titles are distributed in the United States by Slawson Communications Inc., 165 Vallecitos de Oro, San Marcos, CA92069 and are priced at $8.95 each.